To
Our little angel AVA

Merry Christmas 2008!

love,

Grandma + Grandpa
Bragg Creek

Bruno Munari's

ABC

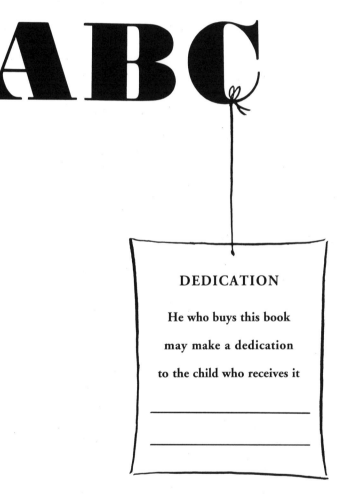

DEDICATION

He who buys this book

may make a dedication

to the child who receives it

_____

_____

Picture books by Bruno Munari

BRUNO MUNARI'S ZOO

ANIMALS FOR SALE

THE BIRTHDAY PRESENT

THE ELEPHANT'S WISH

TIC, TAC, AND TOC

WHO'S THERE?
OPEN THE DOOR!

JIMMY HAS LOST HIS CAP

THE CIRCUS IN THE MIST

chronicle books · san francisco

ABC

by
Bruno
Munari

This edition published in 2006 by Chronicle Books.

Copyright © 1960 by Bruno Munari.
All rights reserved Maurizio Corraini srl - Italy.

Originally published in the United States in 1960
by The World Publishing Company.

Manufactured in Italy.
ISBN-10 0-8118-5463-9
ISBN-13 978-0-8118-5463-4

Library of Congress Catalog Card Number 2002156745

Distributed in Canada by Raincoast Books
9050 Shaughnessy Street, Vancouver, British Columbia V6P 6E5

10 9 8 7 6 5 4 3 2 1

Chronicle Books LLC
85 Second Street, San Francisco, California 94105

www.chroniclekids.com

A

an Ant

on an Apple

a Blue Butterfly

B

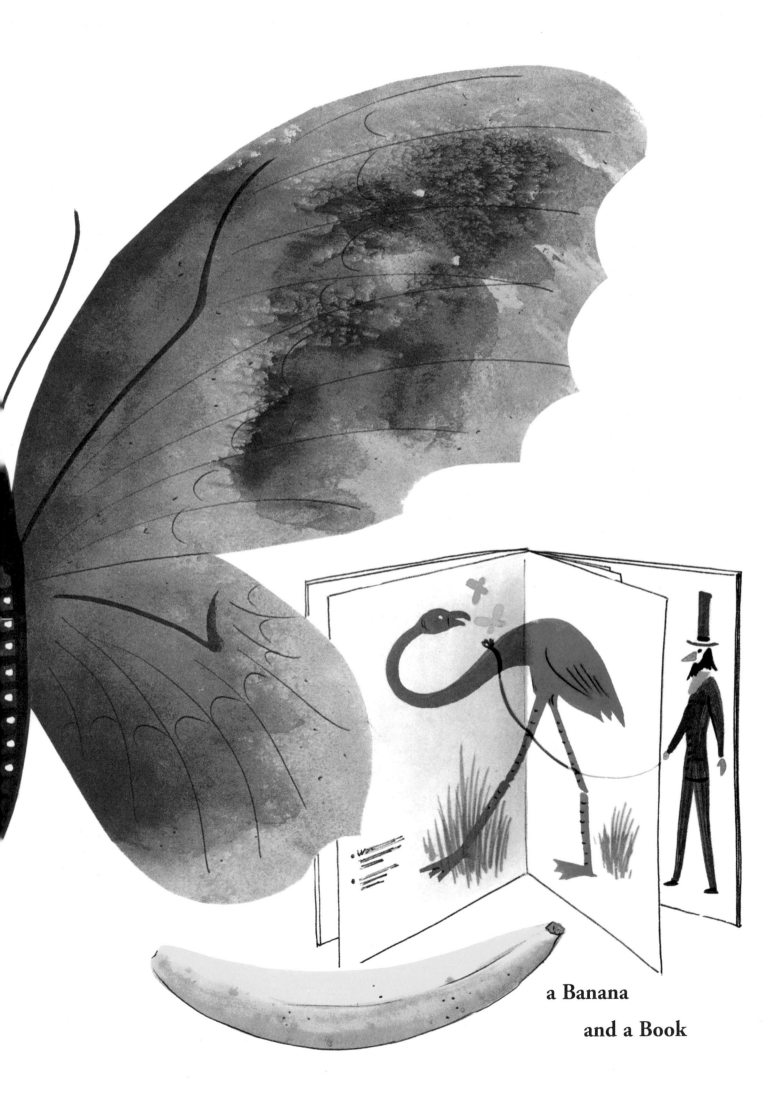

a Banana

and a Book

C

a Crow

on a Cup

a Candle

and a Cat in a Cage

a Drum

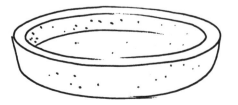

a Dog
and his Dish
outside a Door

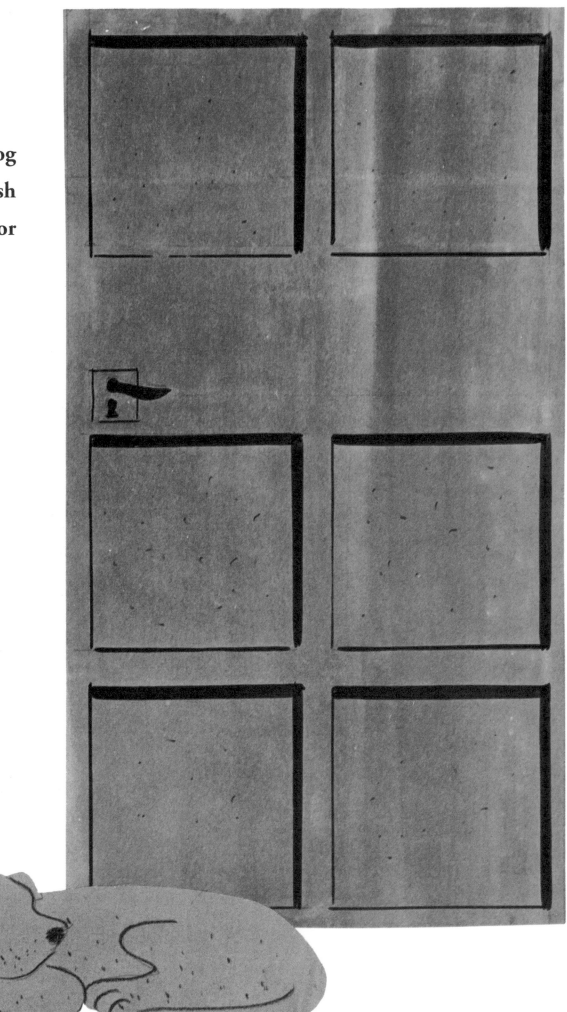

an Elephant

an Egg

an Eye
and an Ear

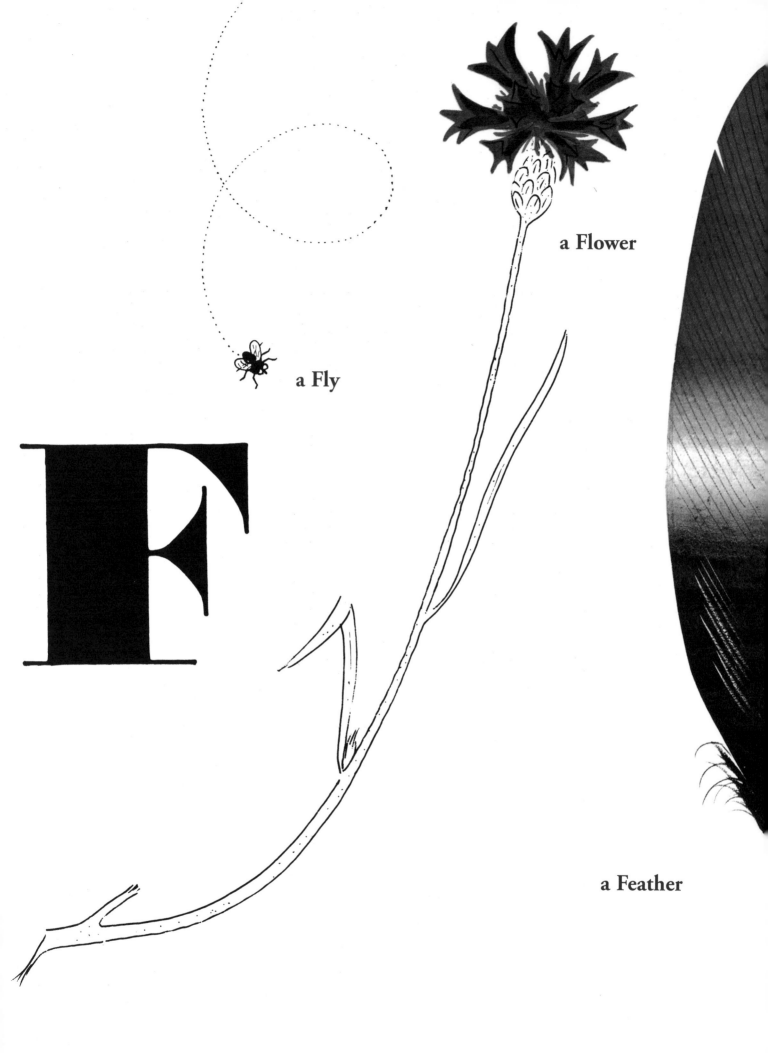

a Flower

a Fly

F

a Feather

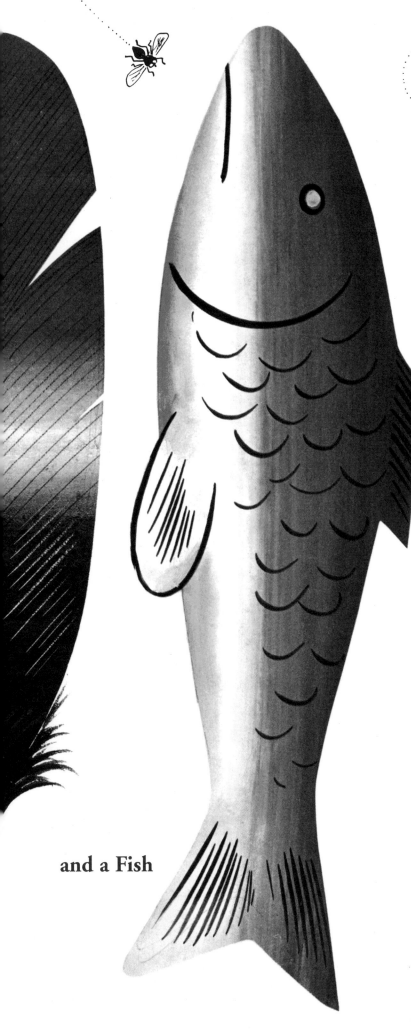

more Flies

and a Fish

G

Glasses in Green Grass

still another fly!

and a Gift for you

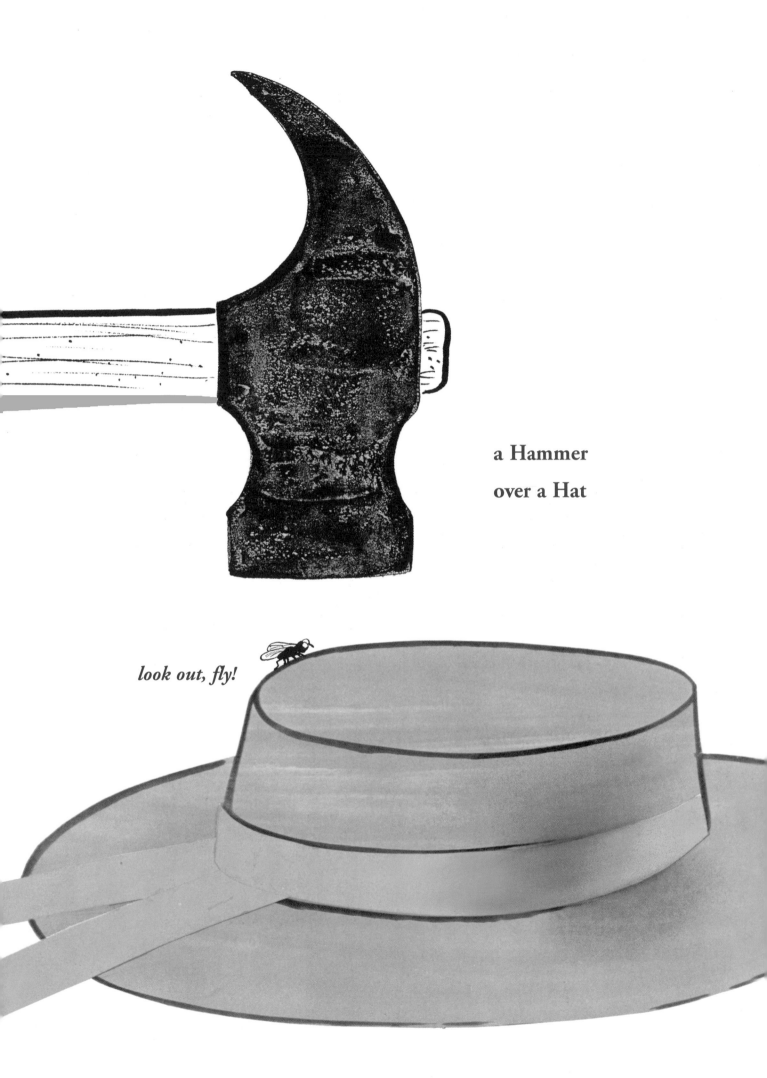

a Hammer
over a Hat

look out, fly!

I

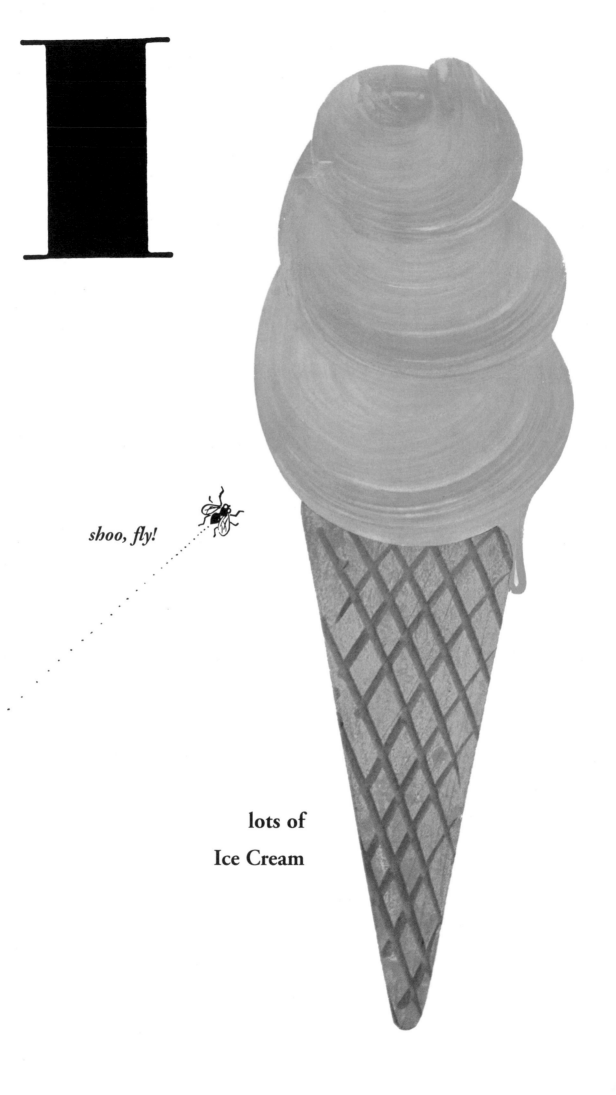

shoo, fly!

lots of
Ice Cream

a Juggler

a Knothole
between a Key
and a Knife

seven Knots on a string and a Kite

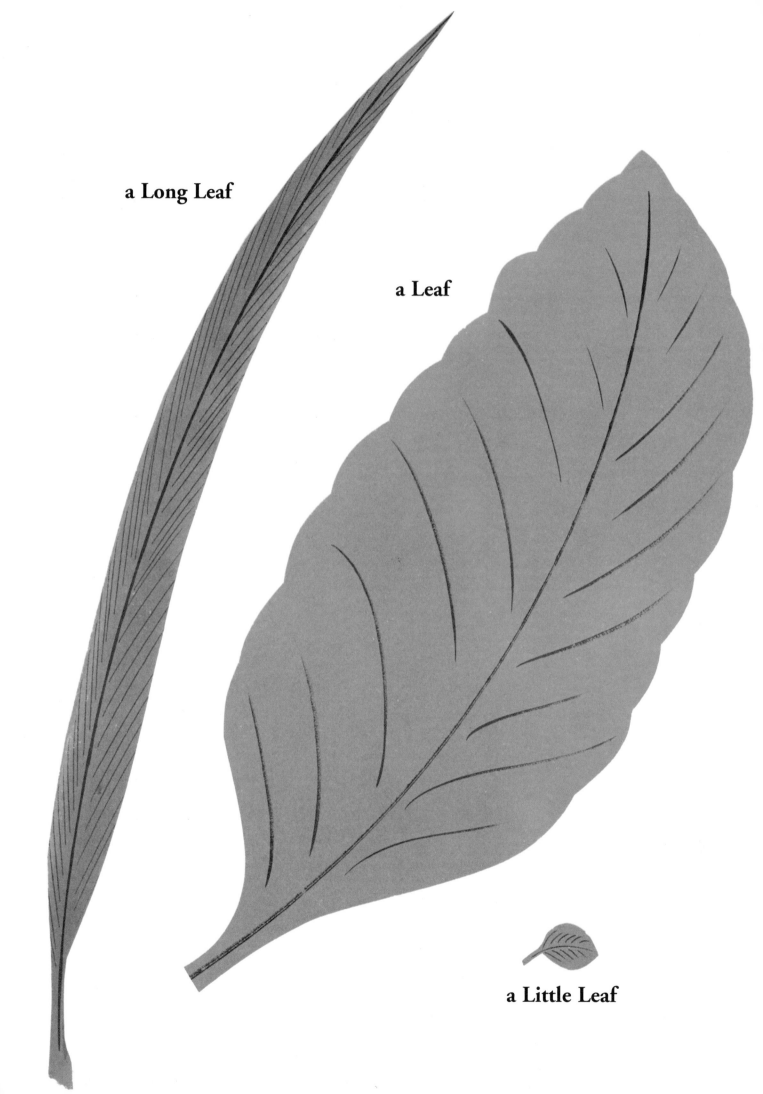

a Long Leaf

a Leaf

a Little Leaf

L

and a Lemon

a Match

M

a Monkey

and a Mouse

No bird in the Nest

N

Nuts on a Nail

an Owl

and an Orange

and an Onion

a Piano

a Package

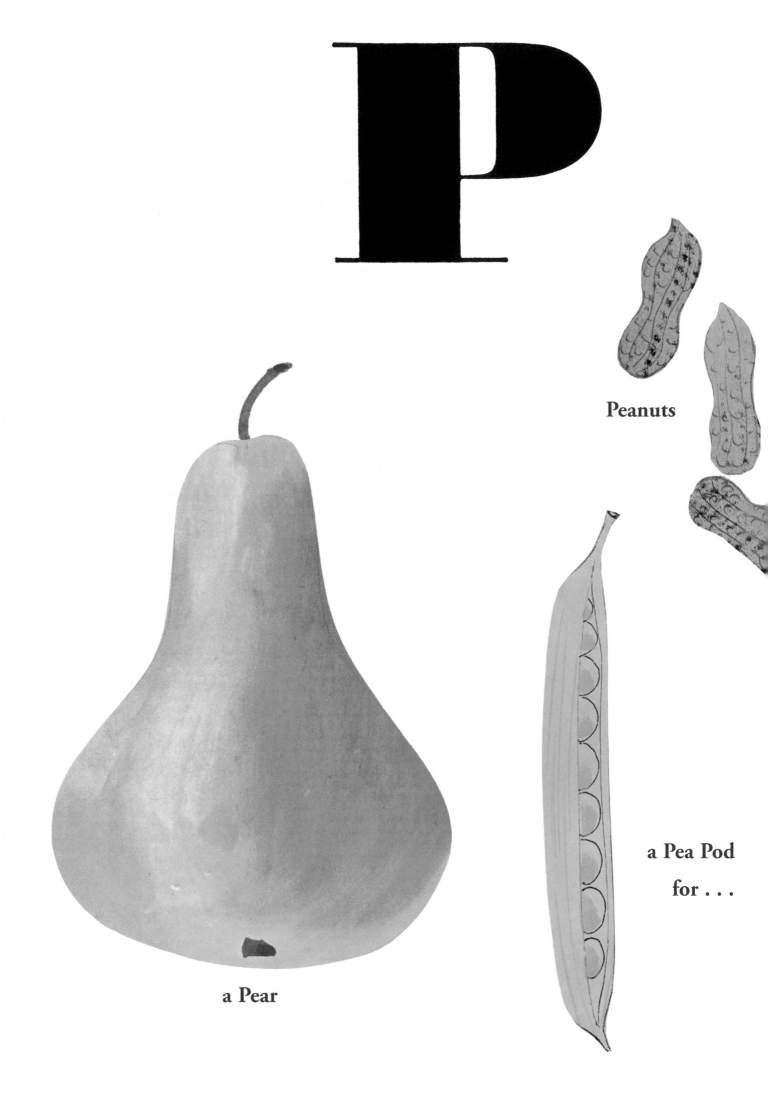

P

Peanuts

a Pear

a Pea Pod
for . . .

a Quail

R

a Rose

and a Red Ribbon

a Sack
of Stars
and Snow
for
Santa Claus

and a Sign

all kinds of Shells

even a Ship

and a Stone

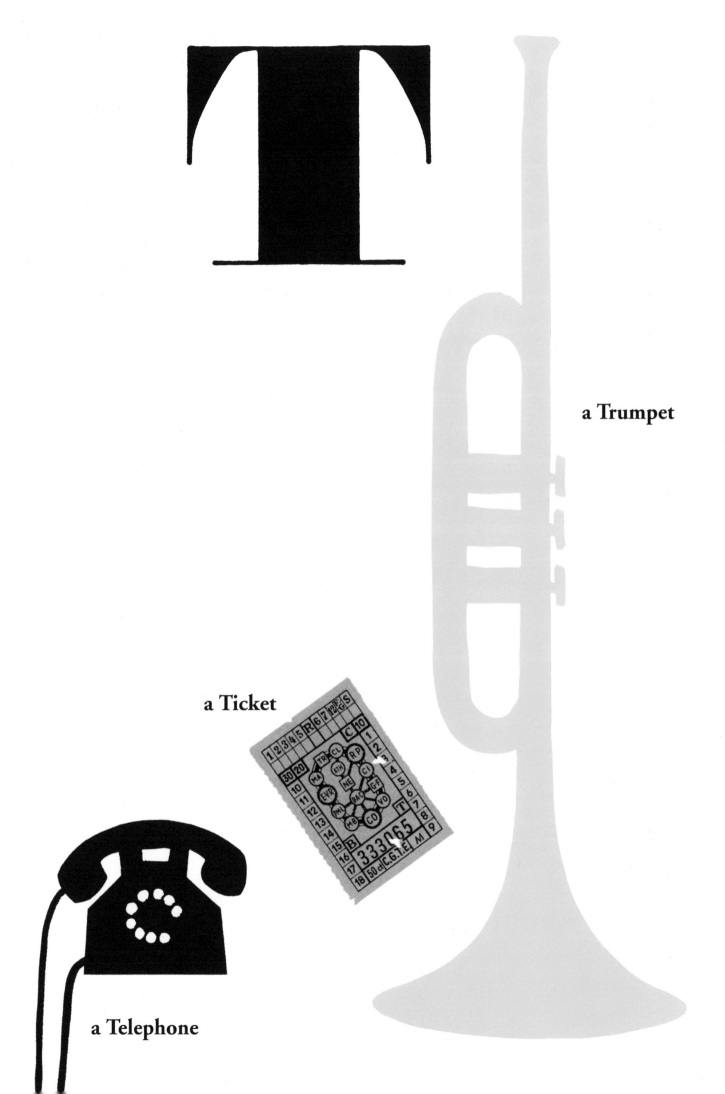

a Trumpet

a Ticket

a Telephone

an Umbrella Up

and an Umbrella

Under the Umbrella

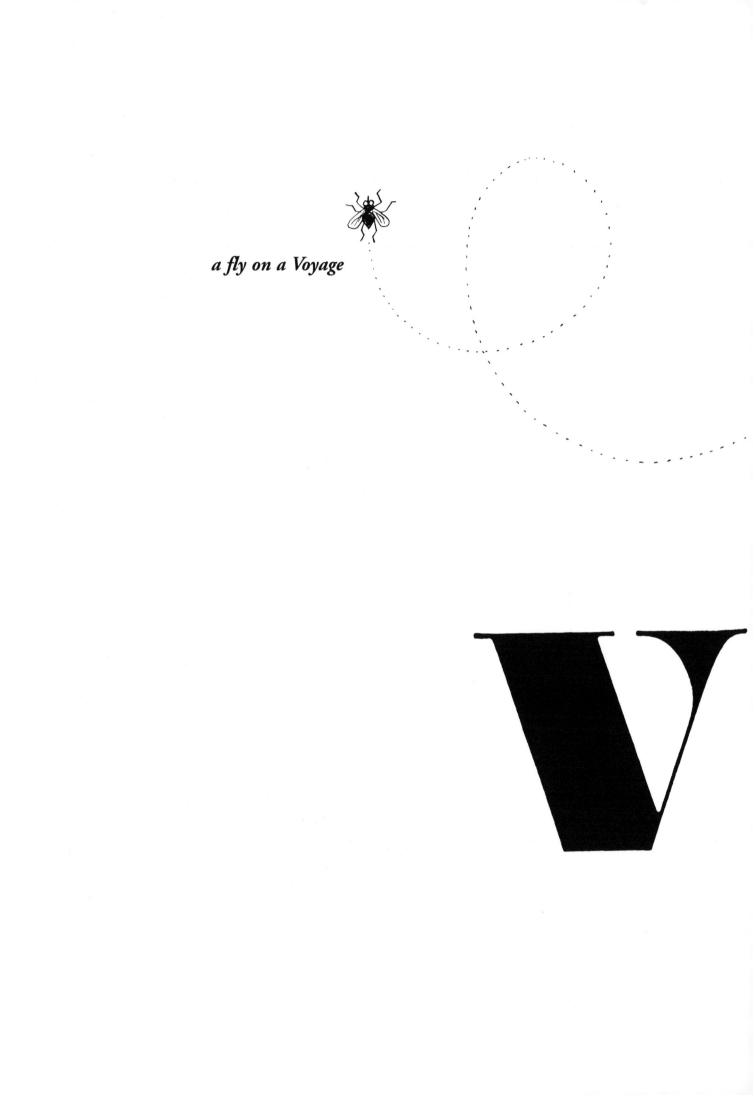

a fly on a Voyage

V

a
Vertical
Violet
Violin

a Watermelon
on a Wagon
with a Wooden Wheel

X

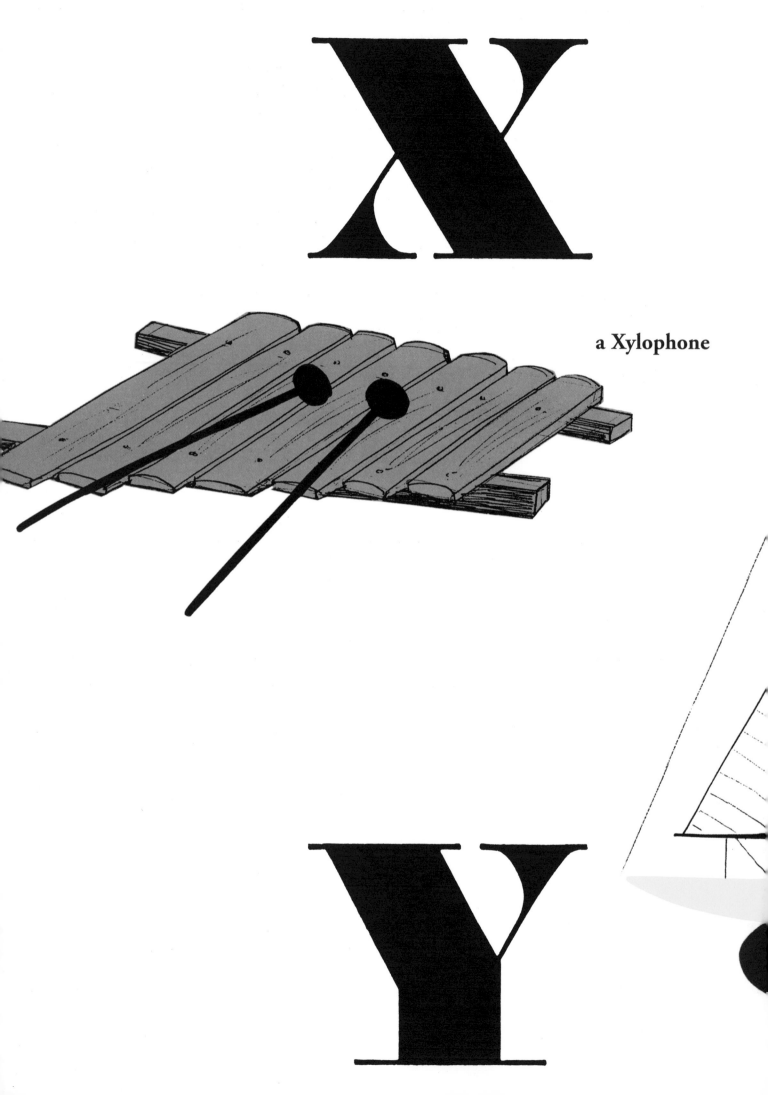

a Xylophone

Y

ZZZZ

ZZZZ

ZZZZ

a Yellow Yacht

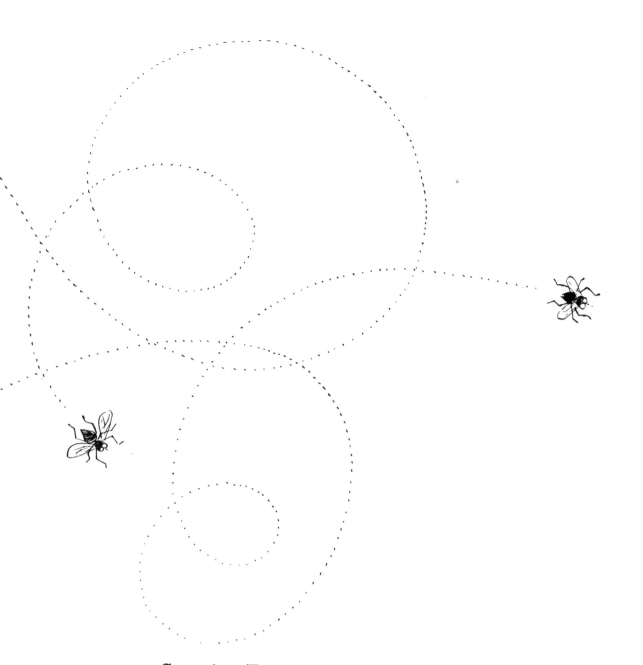

a fly going Zzzz. . . .